VERSES FOR LIFE

LYNDEN N. JONES

I dedicate this book to the individuals who are lost and need guidance to feel empowered, and receive God's love, mercy and the power of His Word.

Acknowledgements

There are countless individuals who have taught me many things in my life both personally and professionally. I could never thank all of you individually, but please know, I have not forgotten who you are, and the contributions you have made to my life.

To my Mom and Aunt - I am grateful for all the sacrifices and difficult decisions you have been faced with throughout my lifetime. I will never be able to truly repay you both. I'm profoundly grateful to have the both of you in my life and could not ask for better parents.

Arlee R. Sheppard - Thanks for your assistance, contribution, energy and time in assisting with research and ensuring that the book was finished.

Contents

PREFACE

This book comprises of a compilation of scriptures and prayers to assist people who are going through problems that may occur in everyday life. The idea came after endless Google searches for Bible verses specific to situations and topics that I have faced in my life such as grief, guilt and illness. This lead me to wonder how many other people, like me, may be going through similar challenges in life and are looking for spiritual guidance. I realized how difficult and time consuming it is to find scriptures in the bible specific to our situation. I decided to share my idea with a couple friends and found out that they too are in need a book like this one. I began to do some research to find out what topics I should use in the book as well as what verses correlated with these topics. After months of research and bible study, I came up with the topics that are enclosed in this book. Hopefully this book helps people who may be going through similar situations as I was. You may be in a season of sorrow, in the middle of a storm, you may be lost and confused but you can always find comfort and guidance from the word of God.

All proceeds from this book shall be used to assist the needy.

Verses To Help In A Of Need

ABORTION

Genesis 9:6

Who so sheds man's blood, by man shall his blood be shed: for in the image of God made he man.

Exodus 20:13

Thou shalt not kill.

Psalm 127:3

Children are a heritage of Jehovah; And the fruit of the womb is his reward.

Psalm 139:13 - 16

(13) For You formed my inward parts; You covered me in my mother's womb. **(14)** I will praise You, for gI am fearfully and wonderfully made; Marvelous are Your works, And that my soul knows very well. **(15)** My frame was not hidden from You, When I was made in secret, And skillfully wrought in the lowest parts of the earth. **(16)** Your eyes saw my substance, being yet unformed. And in Your book they all were written, The days fashioned for me, When as yet there were none of them.

Alcohol Abuse

Ephesians 5:18

And do not get drunk with wine, for that is debauchery, but be filled with the Spirit,

Galatians 5:21

Envying, drunkenness, carousing, and things like these, of which I forewarn you, just as I have forewarned you, that those who practice such things will not inherit the kingdom of God.

Romans 13:13

Let us walk properly as in the daytime, not in orgies and drunkenness, not in sexual immorality and sensuality, not in quarreling and jealousy.

I Corinthians 5:11

But now I am writing to you not to associate with anyone who bears the name of brother if he is guilty of sexual immorality or greed, or is an idolater, reviler, drunkard, or swindler not even to eat with such a one.

I Peter 4:3

For the time already past is sufficient for you to have carried out the desire of the Gentiles, having pursued a course of sensuality, lusts, drunkenness, carousing, drinking parties and abominable idolatries

Anxiety

John 14:27

Peace I leave with you; my peace I give to you. Not as the world gives do I give to you. Let not your hearts be troubled, neither let them be afraid.

Luke 12:25-26

And which of you by being anxious can add a single hour to his span of life? If then you are not able to do as small a thing as that, why are you anxious about the rest?

Matthew 6: 31, 33

(31) So don't worry, saying, 'What will we eat? ' or 'What will we drink? ' or 'What will we wear?

(33) But seek first the kingdom of God and His righteousness, and all these things will be provided for you.

Philippians 4:6 - 7

(6) Don't worry about anything, but in everything, everything, through prayer and petition with thanksgiving, let your requests be made known to God. **(7)** And the peace of God, which surpasses every thought, will guard your hearts and minds in Christ Jesus.

Psalm 46:1

God is our refuge and strength, a helper who is always found in times of trouble.

I Peter 5:7 casting all your anxiety upon him, because he care for you.

Being Lazy

Ephesians 5:16

Making the most of your time, because the days are evil.

Proverbs 6:6 - 11

(6) Go to the ant, O sluggard; consider her ways, and be wise. **(7)** Without having any chief, officer, or ruler, **(8)** she prepares her bread in summer and gathers her food in harvest. **(9)** How long will you lie there, O sluggard?When will you arise from your sleep? **(10)** A little sleep, a little slumber, a little folding of the hands to rest, **(11)** and poverty will come upon you like a robber, and want like an armed man.

Proverbs 13:4

The soul of the sluggard craves and gets nothing, while the soul of the diligent is richly supplied.

Proverbs 20:4

The sluggard does not plow after the autumn, So he begs during the harvest and has nothing.

II Thessalonians 3:10 - 12

(10) For even when we were with you, we would give you this command: If anyone is not willing to work, let him not eat. **(11)** For we hear that some among you walk in idleness, not busy at work, but busybodies. **(12)** Now such persons we command and encourage in the Lord Jesus Christ to do their work quietly and to earn their own living.

Curious About God

John 1:1 - 4

(1) In the beginning was the Word, and the Word was with God, and the Word was God. **(2)** He was with God in the beginning. **(3)** All things were created through Him, and apart from Him not one thing was created that has been created. **(4)** Life was in Him, and that life was the light of men.

John 14:6

Jesus told him, "I am the way, the truth, and the life. No one comes to the Father except through Me.

James 1:5

Now if any of you lacks wisdom, he should ask God, who gives to all generously and without criticizing, and it will be given to him.

Dealing with Abuse

Ephesians 6:4

And, ye fathers, provoke not your children to wrath: but nurture them in the chastening and admonition of the Lord.

Mark 9:42

"But whoever causes the downfall of one of these little ones who believe in Me to stumble it would be better for him if a heavy millstone were hung around his neck and he were thrown into the sea."

Psalm 11:5

The Lord tests the righteous and the wicked, And the one who loves violence His soul hates.

I Corinthians 7:2 - 3

(2) But because sexual immorality is so common, each man should have his own wife, and each woman should have her own husband. **(3)** A husband should fulfill his marital responsibility to his wife, and likewise a wife to her husband.

Dealing With Adversity

James 1:2 - 4

(2) Count it all joy, my brethren, when ye fall into manifold temptations; **(3)** knowing that the proving of your faith works patience. **(4)** And let patience have its perfect work, that ye may be perfect and entire, lacking in nothing.

Philippians 4:6 - 7

(6) Be anxious for nothing, but in everything by prayer and supplication, with thanksgiving, let your requests be made known to God; **(7)**and the peace of God, which surpasses all understanding, will guard your hearts and minds through Christ Jesus.

I Peter 1:6 - 7

(6) In this you rejoice, though now for a little while, if necessary, you have been grieved by various trials, **(7)** so that the tested genuineness of your faith—more precious than gold that perishes though it is tested by fire—may be found to result in praise and glory and honor at the revelation of Jesus Christ.

DEALING WITH CRITICISM

James 5:9

Murmur not, brethren, one against another, that ye be not judged: behold, the judge stand before the doors.

James 4: 11 - 12

(11) Speak not one against another, brethren. He that speak against a brother, or judge his brother, speak against the law, and judge the law: but if thou judges the law, thou art not a doer of the law, but a judge. **(12)** One only is the lawgiver and judge, even he who is able to save and to destroy: but who art thou that judge thy neighbor?

Luke 6: 37 - 42

(37) And judge not, and ye shall not be judged: and condemn not, and ye shall not be condemned: release, and ye shall be released: **(38)** give, and it shall be given unto you; good measure, pressed down, shaken together, running over, shall they give into your bosom. For with what measure ye mete it shall be measured to you again. **(39)** And he spake also a parable unto them, Can the blind guide the blind? shall they not both fall into a pit? **(40)** The disciple is not above his teacher: but every one when he is perfected shall be as his teacher. **(41)** And why behold thou the mote that is in thy brother's eye, but consider not the beam that is in thine own eye? **(42)** Or how canst thou say to thy brother, Brother, let me cast out the mote that is in thine eye, when thou thyself behold not the beam that is in thine own eye? Thou hypocrite, cast out first the beam out of thine own eye, and then shalt thou see clearly to cast out the mote that is in thy brother's eye.

Matthew 6:14 - 15

(14) "For if you forgive people their wrongdoing, your heavenly Father will forgive you as well. **(15)** But if you don't forgive people, your Father will not forgive your wrongdoing."

Romans 14:10, 13

(10) But you, why do you criticize your brother? Or you, why do you look down on your brother? For we will all stand before the tribunal of God.

(13) Therefore, let us no longer criticize one another. Instead decide never to put a stumbling block or pitfall in your brother's way.

Dealing with Death

Hebrews 9:27

(27) And in as much as it is appointed unto men once to die, and after this cometh judgment

John 3:16

For God so loved the world, that he gave his only begotten Son, that whosoever believe on him should not perish, but have eternal life.

John 11:25

(25) Jesus said to her, "I am the resurrection and the life. The one who believes in Me, even if he dies, will live.

I Corinthians 15: 55-58

(55) Death, where is your victory? Death, where is your sting? (56) Now the sting of death is sin, and the power of sin is the law. (57) But thanks be to God, who gives us the victory through our Lord Jesus Christ! (58) Therefore, my dear brothers, be steadfast, immovable, always excelling in the Lord's work, knowing that your labor in the Lord is not in vain.

I Thessalonians 4:13 - 18

(13) We do not want you to be uninformed, brothers, concerning those who are •asleep, so that you will not grieve like the rest, who have no hope. (14) Since we believe that Jesus died and rose again, in the same way God will bring with Him those who have fallen asleep through Jesus. (15) For we say this to you by a revelation from the Lord: We who are still alive at the Lord's coming will certainly have no advantage over those who have fallen asleep. (16) For the Lord Himself will descend from heaven with a shout, with the archangel's voice, and with the trumpet of God, and the dead in Christ will rise first. (17) Then we who are still alive will be caught up together with them in the clouds to meet the Lord in the air and so we will always be with the Lord. (18) Therefore encourage one another with these words.

Revelation 21:4

He will wipe away every tear from their eyes, and death shall be no more, neither shall there be mourning, nor crying, nor pain anymore, for the former things have passed away.

Dealing with Doubt

Matthew 21:21

And Jesus answered them, "Truly, I say to you, if you have faith and do not doubt, you will not only do what has been done to the fig tree, but even if you say to this mountain, 'Be taken up and thrown into the sea,' it will happen. [SEP]

James 1:6

But let him ask in faith, with no doubting, for the one who doubts is like a wave of the sea that is driven and tossed by the wind.

Dealing with Fear

Isaiah 41:10

Fear not, for I am with you; be not dismayed, for I am your God; I will strengthen you, I will help you, I will uphold you with my righteous right hand.

Psalm 31:24

Be strong, and let your heart take courage, all you who wait for the Lord!

Psalm 34:4

"I sought the Lord, and He answered me and delivered me from all my fears."

Psalm 56:3

"When I am afraid, I will trust in You."

Psalm 91:10

No evil shall be allowed to befall you, no plague come near your tent.

Psalm 121:1 - 2

(1) I lift up my eyes to the hills. From where does my help come? **(2)** My help comes from the Lord, who made heaven and earth.

II Timothy 1:7

"For God has not given us a spirit of fearfulness, but one of power, love, and sound judgment."

Dealing with Stress

Matthew 11:28-30 (28) Come unto me, all ye that labor and are heavy laden, and I will give you rest. **(29)** Take my yoke upon you, and learn of me; for I am meek and lowly in heart: and ye shall find rest unto your souls. **(30)** For my yoke is easy, and my burden is light

Psalm 9:9

Jehovah also will be a high tower for the oppressed, A high tower in times of trouble

Phil 4:11 - 13

(11) Not that I speak in respect of want: for I have learned, in whatsoever state I am, therein to be content. **(12)** I know how to be abased, and I know also how to abound: in everything and in all things have I learned the secret both to be filled and to be hungry, both to abound and to be in want. **(13)** I can do all things in him that strengthen me.

Psalm 27:5

For He will conceal me in His shelter in the day of adversity; He will hide me under the cover of His tent; He will set me high on a rock.

Psalm 30:5

For His anger lasts only a moment, but His favor, a lifetime. Weeping may spend the night, but there is joy in the morning.

Psalm 34:4

I sought Jehovah, and he answered me, And delivered me from all my fears.

Psalm 147:3

He heals the brokenhearted and binds up their wounds.

DEALING WITH WORRIES

Luke 10: 41-42

(41) But the Lord answered and said unto her, Martha, Martha, thou art anxious and troubled about many things: (42) but one thing is needful: for Mary hath chosen the good part, which shall not be taken away from her.

Matthew 6: 25-27

(25) Therefore I say unto you, Be not anxious for your life, what ye shall eat, or what ye shall drink; nor yet for your body, what ye shall put on. Is not the life more than the food, and the body than the raiment? **(26)** Behold the birds of the heaven, that they sow not, neither do they reap, nor gather into barns; and your heavenly Father feed them. Are not ye of much more value than they? **(27)** And which of you by being anxious can add one cubit unto the measure of his life?

Matthew 6:34

Be not therefore anxious for the morrow: for the morrow will be anxious for itself. Sufficient unto the day is the evil thereof.

I Peter 5:6 - 7

(6) Humble yourselves, therefore, under the mighty hand of God, so that He may exalt you at the proper time, **(7)** casting all your care on Him, because He cares about you.

Dependence

John 8:34 - 36

"**(34)** Jesus answered them, I assure you: Everyone who commits sin is a slave of sin. **(35)** A slave does not remain in the household forever, but a son does remain forever. **(36)** Therefore, if the Son sets you free, you really will be free.

James 1:13 - 15

"**(13)** No one undergoing a trial should say, "I am being tempted by God." For God is not tempted by evil, and He Himself doesn't tempt anyone. **(14)** But each person is tempted when he is drawn away and enticed by his own evil desires. **(15)** Then after desire has conceived, it gives birth to sin, and when sin is fully grown, it gives birth to death.

James 4:7

Submit yourselves, then, to God. Resist the devil, and he will flee from you.

Proverbs 14:12

"**(12)** There is a way that seems right to a man, but its end is the way to death."

Titus 2:12

Training us to renounce ungodliness and worldly passions, and to live self-controlled, upright, and godly lives in the present age,

I Corinthians 6:12

"I have the right to do anything," you say- but not everything is beneficial. "I have the right to do anything" -- but I will not be mastered by anything.

I John 2:16

For everything in the world--the lust of the flesh, the lust of the eyes, and the pride of life--comes not from the Father but from the world.

DISHONESTY

Matthew 7:2

For with the judgment you pronounce you will be judged, and with the measure you use it will be measured to you.

Proverbs 11:1

A false balance is an abomination to the LORD, But a just weight is His delight.

Proverbs 12:22

Lying lips are an abomination to the LORD, But those who deal faithfully are His delight.

Proverbs 13:11

Wealth obtained by fraud dwindles, But the one who gathers by labor increases it.

DRIFTING FROM GOD

James 1:12

Blessed is the man that endure temptation; for when he hath been approved, he shall receive the crown of life, which the Lord promised to them that love him.

Psalm 51:1, 10

(1) Be gracious to me, God, according to Your faithful love; according to Your abundant compassion, blot out my rebellion

(10) God, create a clean heart for me and renew a steadfast spirit within me.

II Corinthians 13:5

Try your own selves, whether ye are in the faith; prove your own selves. Or know ye not as to your own selves, that Jesus Christ is in you? unless indeed ye be reprobate.

I John 1:8 - 9

(8) If we say, "We have no sin," we are deceiving ourselves, and the truth is not in us. **(9)** If we confess our sins, He is faithful and righteous to forgive us our sins and to cleanse us from all unrighteousness.

Finding Peace

Jeremiah 29:11

For I know the thoughts that I think toward you, saith Jehovah, thoughts of peace, and not of evil, to give you hope in your latter end.

John 14:1 - 4, 27

" **(1)** Your heart must not be troubled. Believe in God; believe also in Me. **(2)** In My Father's house are many dwelling places; if not, I would have told you. I am going away to prepare a place for you. **(3)** If I go away and prepare a place for you, I will come back and receive you to Myself, so that where I am you may be also. **(4)** You know the way to where I am going."

(27) Peace I leave with you. My peace I give to you. I do not give to you as the world gives. Your heart must not be troubled or fearful.

John 16:33

I have told you these things so that in Me you may have peace. You will have suffering in this world. Be courageous! I have conquered the world."

Numbers 6:26

Jehovah lift up his countenance upon thee, and give thee peace.

Romans 5:1 - 5

(1) Therefore, since we have been declared righteous by faith, we have peace with God through our Lord Jesus Christ. **(2)** We have also obtained access through Him by faith into this grace in which we stand, and we rejoice in the hope of the glory of God.

(3) And not only that, but we also rejoice in our afflictions, because we know that affliction produces endurance, **(4)** endurance produces proven character, and proven character produces hope. **(5)** This hope will not disappoint us, because God's love has been poured out in our hearts through the Holy Spirit who was given to us.

Philippians 4:6 - 7

(6) Don't worry about anything, but in everything, through prayer and petition with thanksgiving, let your requests be made known to God. **(7)** And the peace of God, which surpasses every thought, will guard your hearts and minds in Christ Jesus.

Gossip

Matthew 12:36

I tell you, on the day of judgment people will give account for every careless word they speak,

Ephesians 4:29

Let no corrupting talk come out of your mouths, but only such as is good for building up, as fits the occasion, that it may give grace to those who hear.

James 3:1 - 2

(1) Not many of you should become teachers, my brothers, for you know that we who teach will be judged with greater strictness. **(2)** For we all stumble in many ways. And if anyone does not stumble in what he says, he is a perfect man, able also to bridle his whole body.

Psalm 19:14

Let the words of my mouth and the meditation of my heart be acceptable in your sight, O Lord, my rock and my redeemer.

Psalm 101:5

Whoever slanders his neighbor secretly I will destroy. Whoever has a haughty look and an arrogant heart I will not endure.

Psalm 141:3

Set a guard, O Lord, over my mouth; keep watch over the door of my lips!

Proverbs 20:19

Whoever goes about slandering reveals secrets; therefore do not associate with a simple babbler.

II Corinthians 12:20

For I fear, lest by any means, when I come, I should find you not such as I would, and should myself be found of you such as ye would not; lest by any means there should be strife, jealousy, wraths, factions, backbitings, whisperings, swellings, tumults;

I Peter 4:15

But let none of you suffer as a murderer or a thief or an evildoer or as a meddler.

GUILT

Hebrews 10:17

then he adds,"I will remember their sins and their lawless deeds no more."

Psalm 32:5

I acknowledged my sin to you, and I did not cover my iniquity; I said, "I will confess my transgressions to the Lord," and you forgave the iniquity of my sin.

Proverbs 28:13

Whoever conceals his transgressions will not prosper, but he who confesses and forsakes them will obtain mercy.

HOPELESSNESS

Deuteronomy 31:6

Be strong and of good courage, fear not, nor be affrighted at them: for Jehovah thy God, he it is that doth go with thee; he will not fail thee, nor forsake thee.

Hebrews 10:23

Let us hold fast the confession of our hope without wavering, for he who promised is faithful.

Isaiah 41:10

fear thou not, for I am with thee; [a]be not dismayed, for I am thy God; I will strengthen thee; yea, I will help thee; yea, I will uphold thee with the right hand of my righteousness.

Psalm 147:5

Great is our Lord, and mighty in power; His understanding is infinite.

Human Greed

Ecclesiastes 5:10

He that loves silver shall not be satisfied with silver; nor he that loveth abundance, with increase: this also is vanity.

Luke 12:15, 34

(15) And he said to them, "Take care, and be on your guard against all covetousness, for one's life does not consist in the abundance of his possessions."

(34) For where your treasure is, there will your heart be also.

Matthew 6:19 - 21

(19) "Do not lay up for yourselves treasures on earth, where moth and rust[a] destroy and where thieves break in and steal, **(20)** but lay up for yourselves treasures in heaven, where neither moth nor rust destroys and where thieves do not break in and steal.

(21) For where your treasure is, there your heart will be also.

Proverbs 11:24 - 25

(24) One gives freely, yet grows all the richer; another withholds what he should give, and only suffers want. **(25)** Whoever brings blessing will be enriched, and one who waters will himself be watered.

Proverbs 15:27

Whoever is greedy for unjust gain troubles his own household, but he who hates bribes will live.

Proverbs 23:4 - 5

(4) Do not toil to acquire wealth; be discerning enough to desist. **(5)** When your eyes light on it, it is gone, for suddenly it sprouts wings, flying like an eagle toward heaven.

I John 2:16

For all that is in the world, the lust of the flesh and the lust of the eyes and the vainglory of life, is not of the Father, but is of the world.

I Timothy 6:10

For the love of money is a root of all kinds of evils. It is through this craving that some have wandered away from the faith and pierced themselves with many pangs.

ILLNESS

James 5:14 - 15

(14) Is anyone among you sick? He should call for the elders of the church, and they should pray over him after anointing him with olive oil in the name of the Lord. **(15)** The prayer of faith will save the sick person, and the Lord will restore him to health; if he has committed sins, he will be forgiven.

Psalm 41:3

Jehovah will support him upon the couch of languishing: Thou makes all his bed in his sickness.

II Corinthians 12:9 -10

(9) But He said to me, "My grace is sufficient for you, for power is perfected in weakness." Therefore, I will most gladly boast all the more about my weaknesses, so that Christ's power may reside in me. **(10)** So I take pleasure in weaknesses, insults, catastrophes, persecutions, and in pressures, because of Christ. For when I am weak, then I am strong.

INSECURITY

John 10:27 - 28

(27) My sheep hear my voice, and I know them, and they follow me. **(28)** I give them eternal life, and they will never perish, and no one will snatch them out of my hand.

Philippians 4: 6 - 9

(6) In nothing be anxious; but in everything by prayer and supplication with thanksgiving let your requests be made known unto God. **(7)** And the peace of God, which passeth all understanding, shall guard your hearts and your thoughts in Christ Jesus. **(8)** Finally, brethren, whatsoever things are true, whatsoever things are honorable, whatsoever things are just, whatsoever things are pure, whatsoever things are lovely, whatsoever things are of good report; if there be any virtue, and if there be any praise, think on these things. **(9)** The things which ye both learned and received and heard and saw in me, these things do: and the God of peace shall be with you.

I John 4:18

There is no fear in love: but perfect love casteth out fear, because fear hath punishment; and he that fears is not made perfect in love.

Loneliness

Genesis 2:18

And Jehovah God said, It is not good that the man should be alone; I will make him a help meet for him.

Psalm 23

(1) The Lord is my shepherd; there is nothing I lack. **(2)** He lets me lie down in green pastures; He leads me beside quiet waters. **(3)** He renews my life; He leads me along the right paths for His name's sake. **(4)** Even when I go through the darkest valley, I fear no danger, for You are with me; Your rod and Your staff they comfort me. **(5)** You prepare a table before me in the presence of my enemies; You anoint my head with oil; my cup overflows. **(6)** Only goodness and faithful love will pursue me all the days of my life, and I will dwell in the house of the Lord as long as I live.

Psalm 27:10

Even if my father and mother abandon me, the Lord cares for me.

Psalm 143:8

Let me experience Your faithful love in the morning, for I trust in You. Reveal to me the way I should go because I long for You.

Hebrews 13:5

Your life should be free from the love of money. Be satisfied with what you have, for He Himself has said, I will never leave you or forsake you.

1 Peter 5:7

7 casting all your care on Him, because He cares about you.

LUST

Galatians 5:16

But I say, Walk by the Spirit, and ye shall not fulfil the lust of the flesh.

Matthew 5:27-28

(27) Ye have heard that it was said, Thou shalt not commit adultery: **(28)** but I say unto you, that every one that looks on a woman to lust after her hath committed adultery with her already in his heart.

I John 2:15 - 17

(15) Do not love the world or the things in the world. If anyone loves the world, the love of the Father is not in him. **(16)** For all that is in the world—the desires of the flesh and the desires of the eyes and pride of life is not from the Father but is from the world. **(17)** And the world is passing away along with its desires, but whoever does the will of God abides forever.

LYING

Ephesians 4:25

Therefore, having put away falsehood, let each one of you speak the truth with his neighbor, for we are members one of another.

James 5:12

But above all, my brothers, do not swear, either by heaven or by earth or by any other oath, but let your "yes" be yes and your "no" be no, so that you may not fall under condemnation.

Psalm 34:13

Keep thy tongue from evil, And thy lips from speaking guile.

Proverbs 12:19

Truthful lips endure forever, but a lying tongue is but for a moment.

Proverbs 14:5

A faithful witness does not lie, but a false witness breathes out lies

Zechariah 8:16

These are the things that ye shall do: Speak ye every man the truth with his neighbor; execute the judgment of truth and peace in your gates;

Overcoming Adultery

Luke 16:18

Every one that puts away his wife, and marries another, commits adultery: and he that marries one that is put away from a husband commits adultery.

Matthew 5:27 - 28, 31 - 32

(27)" You have heard that it was said ito those of old,' You shall not commit adultery.' (28)" But I say to you that whoever †looks at a woman to lust for her has already committed adultery with her in his heart.

(31)" Furthermore it has been said,' Whoever divorces his wife, let him give her a certificate of divorce.' (32) " But I say to you that †whoever divorces his wife for any reason except sexual immorality causes her to commit adultery; and whoever marries a woman who is divorced commits adultery.

Matthew 19:3-10

(3) And there came unto him Pharisees, trying him, and saying, Is it lawful for a man to put away his wife for every cause? (4) And he answered and said, Have ye not read, that he who made them from the beginning made them male and female, (5) and said, For this cause shall a man leave his father and mother, and shall cleave to his wife; and the two shall become one flesh? (6) So that they are no more two, but one flesh. What therefore God hath joined together, let not man put asunder. (7) They say unto him, Why then did Moses command to give a bill of divorcement, and to put her away? (8) He saith unto them, Moses for your hardness of heart suffered you to put away your wives: but from the beginning it hath not been so. (9) And I say unto you, Whosoever shall put away his wife, except for fornication, and shall marry another, commit adultery: [g]and he that married her when she is put away committed adultery. (10) The disciples say unto him, If the case of the man is so with his wife, it is not expedient to marry.

Proverbs 13:4

The soul of the sluggard craves and gets nothing, while the soul of the diligent is richly supplied.

I Corinthians 6:18

Flee sexual immorality. Every sin that a man does is outside the body, but he who commits sexual immorality sins against his own body.

Overcoming Anger Problems

Ephesians 4:25 - 27

BE ANGRY, AND yet DO NOT SIN; do not let the sun go down on your anger, and do not give the devil an opportunity. Therefore, laying aside falsehood, SPEAK TRUTH EACH ONE of you WITH HIS NEIGHBOR, for we are members of one another.

James 1:20

for the anger of man does not achieve the righteousness of God.

Romans 12:17 - 18, 21

(17) Repay no one evil for evil, but give thought to do what is honorable in the sight of all. **(18)** If possible, so far as it depends on you, live peaceably with all.

(21) Do not be overcome by evil, but overcome evil with good.

Proverbs 15:1

A soft answer turns away wrath, but a harsh word stirs up anger.

Proverbs 19:11

Good sense makes one slow to anger, and it is his glory to overlook an offense.

Proverbs 22:24

Do not associate with a man given to anger; Or go with a hot-tempered man,

Proverbs 29:11

A fool always loses his temper, But a wise man holds it back.

Overcoming Bitterness

Colossians 3:19

Husbands, love your wives and don't be bitter toward them.

Ephesians 4:31 - 32

(31) Let all bitterness, and wrath, and anger, and clamor, and railing, be put away from you, with all malice: **(32)** and be ye kind one to another, tenderhearted, forgiving each other, even as God also in Christ forgave you.

Hebrews 12:14 - 15

(14) Pursue peace with everyone, and holiness, without it no one will see the Lord. **(15)** Make sure that no one falls short of the grace of God and that no root of bitterness springs up, causing trouble and by it, defiling many.

Overcoming Depression

Psalm 3:3 - 5

(3) But you, O Lord, are a shield about me, my glory, and the lifter of my head. (4) I cried aloud to the Lord and he answered me from his holy hill. (5) I lay down and slept;I woke again, for the Lord sustained me. Selah

Psalm 30:5

For his anger is but for a moment, and his favor is for a lifetime. Weeping may tarry for the night, but joy comes with the morning.

Psalm 30:11

Thou hast turned for me my mourning into dancing; Thou hast loosed my sackcloth, and girded me with gladness;

Psalm 34:4

I sought the Lord, and He answered me and delivered me from all my fears.

Psalm 40:1 - 2

(1) I waited patiently for the Lord, and He turned to me and heard my cry for help. (2) He brought me up from a desolate pit, out of the muddy clay, and set my feet on a rock, making my steps secure.

Psalm 42:11

Why are you cast down, O my soul, and why are you in turmoil within me? Hope in God; for I shall again praise him, my salvation and my God.

Psalm 43:5

Why am I so depressed? Why this turmoil within me? Put your hope in God, for I will still praise Him, my Savior and my God.

Psalm 147:3

He heals the brokenhearted and binds up their wounds.

Overcoming Life's Trouble

Psalm 20:1-2

(1) May Yahweh answer you in a day of trouble; may the name of Jacob's God protect you. (2) May He send you help from the sanctuary and sustain you from Zion.

Psalms 23

(1) The Lord is my shepherd; there is nothing I lack. (2) He lets me lie down in green pastures; He leads me beside quiet waters. (3) He renews my life; He leads me along the right paths for His name's sake. (4) Even when I go through the darkest valley, I fear no danger, for You are with me; Your rod and Your staff they comfort me. (5) You prepare a table before me in the presence of my enemies; You anoint my head with oil; my cup overflows. (6) Only goodness and faithful love will pursue me all the days of my life, and I will dwell in the house of the Lord as long as I live.

Psalm 71:1 - 2

(1) Lord, I seek refuge in You; let me never be disgraced. (2) In Your justice, rescue and deliver me; listen closely to me and save me.

OVERCOMING SUICIDAL THOUGHTS

Ecclesiastes 7:17

Do not be over wicked, and do not be a fool– why die before your time?

Ephesians 5:29

After all, no one ever hated their own body, but they feed and care for their body, just as Christ does the church.

Psalm 143:7 - 11

(7) Answer me quickly, Lord; my spirit fails. Don't hide Your face from me, or I will be like those going down to the Pit. **(8)** Let me experience Your faithful love in the morning, for I trust in You. Reveal to me the way I should go because I long for You. **(9)** Rescue me from my enemies, Lord; I come to You for protection. **(10)** Teach me to do Your will, for You are my God. May Your gracious Spirit lead me on level ground. **(11)** Because of Your name, Yahweh, let me live. In Your righteousness deliver me from trouble,

Parting From Your Parents

Ephesians 5:31

For this cause shall a man leave his father and mother, and shall cleave to his wife; and the two shall become one flesh.

Genesis 2:24

Therefore shall a man leave his father and his mother, and shall cleave unto his wife: and they shall be one flesh.

Matthew 19:5

and said, [a]For this cause shall a man leave his father and mother, and shall cleave to his wife; and the two shall become one flesh?

Psalm 139:1 - 3

(1) Lord, You have searched me and known me. (2) You know when I sit down and when I stand up; You understand my thoughts from far away. (3) You observe my travels and my rest; You are aware of all my ways.

Proverbs 3:5 - 6

(5) Trust in the Lord with all your heart, and do not rely on your own understanding;

(6) think about Him in all your ways, and He will guide you on the right paths.

Proverbs 7:1 - 3

(1) My son, obey my words, and treasure my commands. (2) Keep my commands and live; protect my teachings as the pupil of your eye. (3) Tie them to your fingers; write them on the tablet of your heart.

PEER PRESSURE

Ephesians 5:11

Do not participate in the unfruitful deeds of darkness, but instead even expose them;

Exodus 23:2

"You shall not follow the masses in doing evil, nor shall you testify in a dispute so as to turn aside after a multitude in order to pervert justice;

Mark 15:15

Wishing to satisfy the crowd, Pilate released Barabbas for them, and after having Jesus scourged, he handed Him over to be crucified.

Proverbs 1:10 - 15

(10) My son, if sinners entice you, do not consent. **(11)** If they say, "Come with us, let us lie in wait for blood; let us ambush the innocent without reason;**(12)** like Sheol let us swallow them alive, and whole, like those who go down to the pit; **(13)** we shall find all precious goods, we shall fill our houses with plunder; **(14)** throw in your lot among us; we will all have one purse" **(15)** my son, do not walk in the way with them; hold back your foot from their paths,

Proverbs 18:24

A man of too many friends comes to ruin, But there is a friend who sticks closer than a brother.

Psalm 1:1 - 2

(1)Blessed is the man who walks not in the counsel of the wicked, nor stands in the way of sinners, nor sits in the seat of scoffers; **(2)** but his delight is in the law[b] of the Lord, and on his law he meditates day and night.

I Corinthians 15:33

Do not be deceived: "Bad company ruins good morals."

Relationships

Proverbs 13:20

The one who walks with the wise will become wise, but a companion of fools will suffer harm.

Proverbs 17:17

A friend loves at all times, and a brother is born for a difficult time.

Proverbs 18:24

A man with many friends may be harmed, but there is a friend who stays closer than a brother.

Proverbs 31:10-11

(10) A worthy woman who can find? For her price is far above rubies. **(11)** The heart of her husband trust in her, And he shall have no lack of gain.

I Corinthians 15:33

Do not be deceived: "Bad company corrupts good morals."

Resisting Temptation

I Corinthians 10:12 - 13

(12) So, whoever thinks he stands must be careful not to fall. **(13)** No temptation has overtaken you except what is common to humanity. God is faithful, and He will not allow you to be tempted beyond what you are able, but with the temptation He will also provide a way of escape so that you are able to bear it.

James 4:7

Therefore, submit to God. But resist the Devil, and he will flee from you.

I Timothy 6:11

But you, man of God, run from these things, and pursue righteousness, godliness, faith, love, endurance, and gentleness.

REVENGE

Matthew 5:38 - 39

(38) Ye have heard that it was said, An eye for an eye, and a tooth for a tooth: **(39)** but I say unto you, Resist not him that is evil: but whosoever smite thee on thy right cheek, turn to him the other also.

Matthew 5:44

But I say to you, Love your enemies and pray for those who persecute you,

Romans 12:17-21

(17) Render to no man evil for evil. Take thought for things honorable in the sight of all men. **(18)** If it be possible, as much as in you lie, be at peace with all men. **(19)** Avenge not yourselves, beloved, but give place unto the wrath of God: for it is written, Vengeance belong unto me; I will recompense, saith the Lord. **(20)** But if thine enemy hunger, feed him; if he thirst, give him to drink: for in so doing thou shalt heap coals of fire upon his head. **(21)** Be not overcome of evil, but overcome evil with good.

1 Thessalonians 5:15

See that no one repays anyone evil for evil, but always seek to do good to one another and to everyone.

Self -Righteouness

Luke 18:9-14

(9) And he spake also this parable unto certain who trusted in themselves that they were righteous, and set all others at nought: (10) Two men went up into the temple to pray; the one a Pharisee, and the other a publican. (11) The Pharisee stood and prayed thus with himself, God, I thank thee, that I am not as the rest of men, extortioners, unjust, adulterers, or even as this publican. (12) I fast twice in the week; I give tithes of all that I get. (13) But the publican, standing afar off, would not lift up so much as his eyes unto heaven, but smote his breast, saying, God, be thou merciful to me a sinner. (14) I say unto you, This man went down to his house justified rather than the other: for every one that exalt himself shall be humbled; but he that humbles himself shall be exalted.

Philippians 2:3

Do nothing from selfishness or empty conceit, but with humility of mind regard one another as more important than yourselves;

Proverbs 30:12

There is a kind who is pure in his own eyes, Yet is not washed from his filthiness.

I John 1:8

If we say that we have no sin, we are deceiving ourselves and the truth is not in us.

Sexual Immorality

Ephesians 5:3

But fornication, and all uncleanness, or covetousness, let it not even be named among you, as become saints.

Hebrews 13:4

Let marriage be had in honor among all, and let the bed be undefiled: for fornicators and adulterers God will judge.

Matthew 5:27 - 28

(27) "You have heard that it was said, Do not commit adultery. **(28)** But I tell you, everyone who looks at a woman to lust for her has already committed adultery with her in his heart.

Romans 1:26 - 27

(26) This is why God delivered them over to degrading passions. For even their females exchanged natural sexual relations for unnatural ones. **(27)** The males in the same way also left natural relations with females and were inflamed in their lust for one another. Males committed shameless acts with males and received in their own persons the appropriate penalty of their error.

I Corinthians 6:18 - 20

Run from sexual immorality! "Every sin a person can commit is outside the body." On the contrary, the person who is sexually immoral sins against his own body.

Don't you know that your body is a sanctuary of the Holy Spirit who is in you, whom you have from God? You are not your own, **(20)** for you were bought at a price. Therefore glorify God in your body.

II Corinthians 12:21

lest again when I come my God should humble me before you, and I should mourn for many of them that have sinned heretofore, and repented not of the uncleanness and fornication and lasciviousness which they committed.

I Thessalonians 3:3 - 4

(3) that no man be moved by these afflictions; for yourselves know that hereunto we are appointed. **(4)** For verily, when we were with you, we told you beforehand that we are to suffer affliction; even as it came to pass, and ye know.

II Timothy 2:22

Flee from youthful passions, and pursue righteousness, faith, love, and peace, along with those who call on the Lord from a pure heart.

SIN

Ecclesiastes 12:14

For God will bring every work into judgment, with every hidden thing, whether it be good, or whether it be evil.

John 8:34, 36

(34) Jesus answered them, Verily, verily, I say unto you, Every one that commits a sin is the bondservant of sin.

(36) If therefore the Son shall make you free, ye shall be free indeed.

Numbers 32:23

But if ye will not do so, behold, ye have sinned against Jehovah; and be sure your sin will find you out.

Romans 3:23

for all have sinned, and fall short of the glory of God;

Sorrow (Grief)

Matthew 5:4

Blessed are they that mourn: for they shall be comforted.

Psalms 23

(1) The Lord is my shepherd; there is nothing I lack. (2) He lets me lie down in green pastures; He leads me beside quiet waters. (3) He renews my life; He leads me along the right paths for His name's sake. (4) Even when I go through the darkest valley, I fear no danger, for You are with me; Your rod and Your staff they comfort me. (5) You prepare a table before me in the presence of my enemies; You anoint my head with oil; my cup overflows. (6) Only goodness and faithful love will pursue me all the days of my life, and I will dwell in the house of the Lord as long as I live.

Psalm 34:18

The Lord is near the brokenhearted; He saves those crushed in spirit.

Psalm 147:3

He heals the brokenhearted and binds up their wounds.

Revelation 21:4

and he shall wipe away every tear from their eyes; and death shall be no more; neither shall there be mourning, nor crying, nor pain, any more: the first things are passed away.

II Corinthians 1:3 - 4

(3) Praise the God and Father of our Lord Jesus Christ, the Father of mercies and the God of all comfort. (4) He comforts us in all our affliction, so that we may be able to comfort those who are in any kind of affliction, through the comfort we ourselves receive from God.

Stealing

Ephesians 4:28

Let him that stole steal no more: but rather let him labor, working with his hands the thing that is good, that he may have whereof to give to him that hath need.

Exodus 20:15

Thou shalt not steal.

Leviticus 19:11

Ye shall not steal, neither deal falsely, neither lie one to another.

Proverbs 29:24

Whoever is partner with a thief hates his own soul; if he hears the adjuration and utters nothing.

I Peter 4:15

For let none of you suffer as a murderer, or a thief, or an evil-doer, or as a meddler in other men's matters.

Swearing

Colossians 3:8

but now do ye also put them all away: anger, wrath, malice, railing, shameful speaking out of your mouth:

Genesis 49:7

Cursed be their anger, for it was fierce; And their wrath, for it was cruel: I will divide them in Jacob, And scatter them in Israel.

Exodus 22:28

Thou shalt not revile [a]God, nor curse a ruler of thy people.

Ephesians 4:29

Let no corrupt speech proceed out of your mouth, but such as is good for edifying as the need may be, that it may give grace to them that hear.

Matthew 15:11

"It is not what enters into the mouth that defiles the man, but what proceeds out of the mouth, this defiles the man."

WRONG DOINGS

Isaiah 55:7

 let the wicked forsake his way, and the unrighteous man his thoughts; and let him return unto Jehovah, and he will have mercy upon him; and to our God, for he will abundantly pardon.

Psalm 51:1

Be gracious to me, God, according to Your faithful love; according to Your abundant compassion, blot out my rebellion.

Proverbs 28:13

The one who conceals his sins will not prosper, but whoever confesses and renounces them will find mercy.

I John 1:9

If we confess our sins, He is faithful and righteous to forgive us our sins and to cleanse us from all unrighteousness.

I John 2:1

My little children, these things write I unto you that ye may not sin. And if any man sin, we have an [a]Advocate with the Father, Jesus Christ the righteous.

WEARY

Mathew 11:28 - 30

(28) "Come to Me, all of you who are weary and burdened, and I will give you rest. (29) All of you, take up My yoke and learn from Me, because I am gentle and humble in heart, and you will find rest for yourselves. (30) For My yoke is easy and My burden is light."

Galatians 6:9

So we must not get tired of doing good, for we will reap at the proper time if we don't give up.

Psalm 105:4

Seek ye Jehovah and his strength; Seek his face evermore.

Psalm 55:22

Cast thy burden upon Jehovah, and he will sustain thee: He will never suffer the righteous to be moved.

Temptation

Matthew 26:41

Watch and pray, that ye enter not into temptation: the spirit indeed is willing, but the flesh is weak.

James 4:7

Be subject therefore unto God; but resist the devil, and he will flee from you.

Psalm, 119:11

Thy word have I laid up in my heart, That I might not sin against thee.

I Corinthians 10:13

There hath no temptation taken you but such as man can bear: but God is faithful, who will not suffer you to be tempted above that ye are able; but will with the temptation make also the way of escape, that ye may be able to endure it.

II Peter 2:9

the Lord knows how to deliver the godly out of temptation, and to keep the unrighteous under punishment unto the day of judgment;

TERROR AND WAR

Exodus 23:27

"I will send My terror ahead of you, and throw into confusion all the people among whom you come, and I will make all your enemies turn their backs to you.

Philippians 4:6 - 7

(6) In nothing be anxious; but in everything by prayer and supplication with thanksgiving let your requests be made known unto God. (7) And the peace of God, which passeth all understanding, shall guard your hearts and your thoughts in Christ Jesus.

Psalm 24:8

Who is the King of glory? Jehovah strong and mighty, Jehovah mighty in battle.

Psalm 37:3 - 7

(3) Trust in Jehovah, and do good; Dwell in the land, and [b]feed on his faithfulness. (4) Delight thyself also in Jehovah; And he will give thee the [d]desires of thy heart.

(5) Commit thy way unto Jehovah; Trust also in him, and he will bring it to pass. (6) And he will make thy righteousness to go forth as the light, And thy justice as the noon-day. (7) Rest in Jehovah, and wait patiently for him: Fret not thyself because of him who prosper in his way, Because of the man who brings the wicked devices to pass.

Verses For A Better Christian Life.

ABUNDANCE

John 10:10

The thief cometh not, but that he may steal, and kill, and destroy: I came that they may have life, and may have it abundantly.

Matthew 4:4

But he answered and said, It is written, Man shall not live by bread alone, but by every word that proceeds out of the mouth of God.

II Corinthians 9:8

And God is able to make all grace abound unto you; that ye, having always all sufficiency in everything, may abound unto every good work

Assurance

John 5:24

Verily, verily, I say unto you, He that hears my word, and believes him that sent me, hath eternal life, and cometh not into judgment, but hath passed out of death into life.

John 6:37

All that which the Father giveth me shall come unto me; and him that cometh to me I will in no wise cast out.

Romans 10:13

for, Whosoever shall call upon the name of the Lord shall be saved

COMPASSION

Ephesians 4:32

And be ye kind one to another, tenderhearted, forgiving each other, even as God also in Christ forgave you.

Jude 1:22

And on some have mercy, who are in doubt;

Mark 6:34

And he came forth and saw a great multitude, and he had compassion on them, because they were as sheep not having a shepherd: and he began to teach them many things.

Psalm 145:8

Jehovah is gracious, and merciful; Slow to anger, and of great lovingkindness.

1 Peter 3:8

Finally, be ye all likeminded, [a]compassionate, loving as brethren, tenderhearted, humble minded:

CONTENTMENT

Philippians 4:11-13

(11) Not that I speak in respect of want: for I have learned, in whatsoever state I am, therein to be content. **(12)** I know how to be abased, and I know also how to abound: in everything and in all things have I learned the secret both to be filled and to be hungry, both to abound and to be in want. **(13)** I can do all things in him that strengthen me.

I Timothy 6 :6-12

(6) But godliness with contentment is great gain: **(7)** for we brought nothing into the world, for neither can we carry anything out; **(8)** but having food and covering we shall be therewith content. **(9)** But they that are minded to be rich fall into a temptation and a snare and many foolish and hurtful lusts, such as drown men in destruction and perdition. **(10)** For the love of money is a root of all kinds of evil: which some reaching after have been led astray from the faith, and have pierced themselves through with many sorrows. **(11)** But thou, O man of God, flee these things; and follow after righteousness, godliness, faith, love, patience, meekness. **(12)** Fight the good fight of the faith, lay hold on the life eternal, whereunto thou wast called, and didst confess the good confession in the sight of many witnesses.

II Corinthians 12:9-10

(9) And he hath said unto me, My grace is sufficient for thee: for my power is made perfect in weakness. Most gladly therefore will I rather glory in my weaknesses, that the power of Christ may [a]rest upon me. **(10)** Wherefore I take pleasure in weaknesses, in injuries, in necessities, in persecutions, in distresses, for Christ's sake: for when I am weak, then am I strong.

Job 36:11

If they hearken and serve him, They shall spend their days in prosperity, And their years in pleasures.

Deuteronomy

31:6 Courage

Be strong and of good courage, do not fear nor be afraid of them; for the LORD your God, He is the One who goes with you. He will not leave you nor forsake you.

Psalm 27:14

Wait for Jehovah: Be strong, and let thy heart take courage; Yea, wait thou for Jehovah.

Psalm 31:24

Be strong, and let your heart take courage, All ye that hope in Jehovah.

I Chronicles 28:20

And David said to Solomon his son, Be strong and of good courage, and do it: fear not, nor be dismayed; for Jehovah God, even my God, is with thee; he will not fail thee, nor forsake thee, until all the work for the service of the house of Jehovah be finished.

I Corinthians 16:13

Watch ye, stand fast in the faith, quit you like men, be strong.

DILIGENCE

Luke 9:62

But Jesus said unto him, No man, having put his hand to the plow, and looking back, is fit for the kingdom of God.

Galatians 6:9

And let us not be weary in well-doing: for in due season we shall reap, if we faint not.

Philippians 3:14

I press on toward the goal unto the prize of the high calling of God in Christ Jesus.

Proverbs 12:24

The hand of the diligent shall bear rule; But the slothful shall be put under task work.

Proverbs 13:4

The soul of the sluggard desires, and hath nothing; But the soul of the diligent shall be made fat.

Proverbs 21:5

The thoughts of the diligent tend only to plenteousness; But every one that is hasty hast only to want.

! Peter 1:10

Wherefore, brethren, give the more diligence to make your calling and election sure: for if ye do these things, ye shall never stumble.

2 Peter 3:14

Wherefore, beloved, seeing that ye look for these things, give diligence that ye may be found in peace, without spot and blameless in his sight.

ENDURANCE

Hebrews 10:32

But call to remembrance the former days, in which, after ye were enlightened, ye endured a great conflict of sufferings;

Hebrews 12:3

For consider him that hath endured such gainsaying of sinners against himself, that ye wax not weary, fainting in your souls.

Isaiah 42:3-4

(3) A bruised reed will he not break, and a dimly burning wick will he not quench: he will bring forth justice in truth. **(4)** He will not fail nor be discouraged, till he have set justice in the earth; and the isles shall wait for his law.

Galatians 6:9

And let us not be weary in well-doing: for in due season we shall reap, if we faint not.

Matthew 24:13

But he that endures to the end, the same shall be saved.

FAITHFULNESS

Deuteronomy 7:9

Know therefore that Jehovah thy God, he is God, the faithful God, who keeps the covenant and lovingkindness with them that love him and keep his commandments to a thousand generations,

Luke 16:10

He that is faithful in a very little is faithful also in much: and he that is unrighteous in a very little is unrighteous also in much.

Psalm 36:5

Thy lovingkindness, O Jehovah, is in the heavens; Thy faithfulness reaches unto the skies.

Psalm 119:90

Thy faithfulness is unto all generations: Thou hast established the earth, and it abide.

Romans 4:20 - 22

(20) yet, looking unto the promise of God, he wavered not through unbelief, but waxed strong through faith, giving glory to God, **(21)** and being fully assured that what he had promised, he was able also to perform. **(22)** Wherefore also it was reckoned unto him for righteousness.

1 Corinthians 1:9

God is faithful, through whom ye were called into the fellowship of his Son Jesus Christ our Lord.

II Thessalonians 3:3

But the Lord is faithful, who shall establish you, and guard you from the evil one.

FORGIVENESS

Acts 2:38

And Peter said unto them, Repent ye, and be baptized every one of you in the name of Jesus Christ unto the remission of your sins; and ye shall receive the gift of the Holy Spirit.

Colossians 3:13

Forbearing one another, and forgiving each other, if any man have a complaint against any; even as the Lord forgave you, so also do ye:

Ephesians 4:32

and be ye kind one to another, tenderhearted, forgiving each other, even as God also in Christ forgave you.

Matthew 6:14-15

14. For if ye forgive men their trespasses, your heavenly Father will also forgive you.

15. But if ye forgive not men their trespasses, neither will your Father forgive your trespasses.

I John 1:9

If we confess our sins, he is faithful and righteous to forgive us our sins, and to cleanse us from all unrighteousness.

Generosity

Luke 6:30

If any of you lacks wisdom, you should ask God, who gives generously to all without finding fault, and it will be given to you.

Proverbs 11:25

The liberal soul shall be made fat; And he that waters it shall be watered also himself.

II Corinthians 8:12

You will be enriched in every way so that you can be generous on every occasion, and through us your generosity will result in thanksgiving to God.

II Corinthians 9:7

Give, and it will be given to you. A good measure, pressed down, shaken together and running over, will be poured into your lap. For with the measure you use, it will be measured to you.

2 Corinthians 9:11

Good will come to those who are generous and lend freely, who conduct their affairs with justice.

Gentleness

Colossians 3:12

Be wise in the way you act toward outsiders; make the most of every opportunity. Let your conversation be always full of grace, seasoned with salt, so that you may know how to answer everyone.

Colossians 4:5-6

A gentle answer turns away wrath, but a harsh word stirs up anger.

Ephesians 4:2

with all lowliness and meekness, with long suffering, forbearing one another in love;

James 3:17

But the wisdom that is from above is first pure, then peaceable, gentle, easy to be entreated, full of mercy and good fruits, without variance, without hypocrisy.

Philippians 4:5

Let your forbearance be known unto all men. The Lord is at hand.

Proverbs 15:1

Gracious words are a honeycomb, sweet to the soul and healing to the bones.

I Timothy 6:11

But thou, O man of God, flee these things; and follow after righteousness, godliness, faith, love, patience, meekness.

GODLINESS

2 Peter 1:2

Grace to you and peace be multiplied in the knowledge of God and of Jesus our Lord

1 Timothy 4:7 - 8

(7) but refuse profane and old wives' fables. And exercise thyself unto godliness: **(8)** for bodily exercise is profitable for a little; but godliness is profitable for all things, having promise of the life which now is, and of that which is to come.

I Timothy 6:6 - 7

(6) But godliness with contentment is great gain. **(7)** For we brought nothing into the world, and we can take nothing out of it.

Good Works

Colossians 1:10

to walk worthily of the Lord unto all pleasing, bearing fruit in every good work, and increasing in the knowledge of God;

Ephesians 2:8 - 10

(8) for by grace have ye been saved through faith; and that not of yourselves, it is the gift of God; (9) not of works, that no man should glory. (10) For we are his workmanship, created in Christ Jesus for good works, which God afore prepared that we should walk in them.

John 15:5, 8

(5) I am the vine, ye are the branches: He that abide in me, and I in him, the same bare much fruit: for apart from me ye can do nothing.

(8) Herein is my Father glorified, that ye bear much fruit; and so shall ye be my disciples.

Titus 3 :1

Put them in mind to be subject to principalities and powers, to obey magistrates, to be ready to every good work

Titus 3 :8

This is a faithful saying, and these things I will that thou affirm constantly, that they which have believed in God might be careful to maintain good works. These things are good and profitable unto men.

Titus 3 :14

And let ours also learn to maintain good works for necessary uses, that they be not unfruitful.

I Timothy 2 :10

But (which become women professing godliness) with good works.

I Timothy 5 :10

Well reported of for good works; if she have brought up children, if she have lodged strangers, if she have washed the saints' feet, if she have relieved the afflicted, if she have diligently followed every good work.

Guidance

Psalm 32:8

I will instruct thee and teach thee in the way which thou shalt go: I will counsel thee with mine eye upon thee.

Psalm 37:5

Commit thy way unto Jehovah; Trust also in him, and he will bring it to pass.

Proverbs 3 :6

In all thy ways acknowledge him, and he shall direct thy paths.

Proverbs 4:20 - 22

20 My son, attend to my words; Incline thine ear unto my sayings. 21 Let them not depart from thine eyes; Keep them in the midst of thy heart. 22 For they are life unto those that find them, And health to all their flesh.

Proverbs 16:3

Commit thy works unto Jehovah, And thy purposes shall be established.

1 Chronicles 10:13

So Saul died for his trespass which he committed against Jehovah, because of the word of Jehovah, which he kept not; and also for that he asked counsel of one that had a familiar spirit, to inquire thereby,

GRATITUDE

Ephesians 5:20

giving thanks always for all things in the name of our Lord Jesus Christ to God, even t h e Fa t h e r

Philippians 4:6

In nothing be anxious; but in everything by prayer and supplication with thanks giving

let your requests be made known unto God

Psalm 100:4

Enter into his gates with thanksgiving, And into his courts with praise: Give thanks unto him, and bless his name.

Psalm 119:165

Great peace have they that love thy law; And they have no occasion of stumbling.

I Corinthians 15:57

But thanks be to God, who giveth us the victory through our Lord Jesus Christ.

I Chronicles 16:34

O give thanks unto Jehovah; for he is good; For his lovingkindness endures for ever.

Happiness

Acts 2:28

Thou made known unto me the ways of life; Thou shalt make me full of gladness with thy countenance.

Psalm 16:11

Thou wilt show me the path of life: In thy presence is fulness of joy; In thy right hand

th ere are p leas u res fo r ever m o re.[SEP]

Psalm 35:9

And my soul shall be joyful in Jehovah: It shall rejoice in his salvation.

Psalm 118:24

This is the day which Jehovah hath made; We will rejoice and be glad in it.

Romans 15:13

Now the God of hope fill you with all joy and peace in believing, that ye may abound in hope, in the power of the Holy Spirit.

Honesty

Matthew 7:2

For with what judgment ye judge, ye shall be judged: and with what measure ye mete, it shall be measured unto you.

Proverbs 11:3

The integrity of the upright shall guide them; But the perverseness of the treacherous shall destroy them.

Proverbs 21:3

To do righteousness and justice Is more acceptable to Jehovah than sacrifice.

Psalm 26:1

Judge me, O Jehovah, for I have walked in mine integrity: I have trusted also in Jehovah without wavering.

I John 3:18

My little children, let us not love in word, neither with the tongue; but in deed and truth.

Hope

Jeremiah 17:7

Blessed is the man that trust in Jehovah, and whose trust Jehovah is.

Romans 5:5

and hope put not to shame; because the love of God hath been shed abroad in our hearts through the Holy Spirit which was given unto us.

Romans 15:13

Now the God of hope fill you with all joy and peace in believing, that ye may abound in hope, in the power of the Holy Spirit.

Psalm 16:9

Therefore my heart is glad, and my glory rejoice: My flesh also shall dwell in safety.

Psalm 31:24

Be strong, and let your heart take courage, All ye that hope in Jehovah.

Psalm 147:11

Jehovah taketh pleasure in them that fear him, In those that hope in his lovingkindness.

HUMILITY

Matthew 18:4

Whosoever therefore shall humble himself as this little child, the same is the greatest in the kingdom of heaven.

Matthew 23:12

And whosoever shall exalt himself shall be humbled; and whosoever shall humble himself shall be exalted.

James 3:13

Who is wise and understanding among you? let him show by his good life his works in meekness of wisdom.

James 4:6 - 10

(6) But he giveth more grace. Wherefore the scripture saith, God resist the proud, but giveth grace to the humble. **(7)** Be subject therefore unto God; but resist the devil, and he will flee from you. **(8)** Draw nigh to God, and he will draw nigh to you. Cleanse your hands, ye sinners; and purify your hearts, ye double minded. **(9)** Be afflicted, and mourn, and weep: let your laughter be turned to mourning, and your joy to heaviness.

(10) Humble yourselves in the sight of the Lord, and he shall exalt you.

Proverbs 15:33

The fear of Jehovah is the instruction of wisdom; And before honor goeth humility.

Proverbs 22:4

The reward of humility and the fear of Jehovah Is riches, and honor, and life.

I Peter 5:6

Humble yourselves therefore under the mighty hand of God, that he may exalt you in due time

KINDNESS

Colossians 3:12 - 14

(12) Put on therefore, as God's elect, holy and beloved, a heart of compassion, kindness, lowliness, meekness, long suffering; **(13)** forbearing one another, and forgiving each other, if any man have a complaint against any; even as the Lord forgave you, so also do ye: **(14)** and above all these things put on love, which is the bond of perfectness.

Ephesians 4:32

and be ye kind one to another, tenderhearted, forgiving each other, even as God also in Christ forgave you.

Galatians 5:22

But the fruit of the Spirit is love, joy, peace, long suffering, kindness, goodness, faithfulness.

Psalm 117:2

For his lovingkindness is great toward us; And the truth of Jehovah endure for ever. Praise ye Jehovah.

Romans 2:4

Or despise thou the riches of his goodness and forbearance and long suffering, not knowing that the goodness of God lead thee to repentance?

LOVE

Deuteronomy 6:5

And thou shalt love Jehovah thy God with all thy heart, and with all thy soul, and with all thy might.

John 13:34 - 35

(34) A new commandment I give unto you, that ye love one another; [a]even as I have loved you, that ye also love one another. (35) By this shall all men know that ye are my disciples, if ye have love one to another.

Lamentations 3:22

It is of Jehovah's loving kindnesses that we are not consumed, because his compassions fail not.

Romans 12:19

Avenge not yourselves, beloved, but give place unto the wrath of God: for it is written, Vengeance belong unto me; I will recompense, saith the Lord.

I Corinthians 13:5

do not behave itself unseemly, seek not its own, is not provoked, taketh not account of evil;

I John 3:1, 11

(1) Behold what manner of love the Father hath bestowed upon us, that we should be called children of God; and such we are. For this cause the world knows us not, because it knew him not.

(11) For this is the message which ye heard from the beginning, that we should love one another.

I John 4:7, 10, 19

(7) Beloved, let us love one another: for love is of God; and every one that loveth is be-gotten of God, and know God.

(10) Herein is love, not that we loved God, but that he loved us, and sent his Son to be the propitiation for our sins.

(19) We love, because he first loved us.

Mercy

Ephesians 2:4

But God, being rich in mercy, for his great love wherewith he loved us,

Hebrews 4:16

Let us therefore draw near with boldness unto the throne of grace, that we may receive mercy, and may find grace to help us in time of need.

Luke 1:50

And his mercy is unto generations and generations On them that fear him.

Matthew 9:13

But go ye and learn what this mean, I desire mercy, and not sacrifice: for I came not to call the righteous, but sinners.

Titus 3:5

Not by works done in righteousness, which we did ourselves, but according to his mercy he saved us, through the [a]washing of regeneration [b]and renewing of the Holy Spirit,

Psalm 25:7

Remember not the sins of my youth, nor my transgressions: According to thy lovingkindness remember thou me, For thy goodness' sake, O Jehovah.

Romans 9:15

For he saith to Moses, I will have mercy on whom I have mercy, and I will have compassion on whom I have compassion.

Obedience

Deuteronomy 28:1

And it shall come to pass, if thou shalt hearken diligently unto the voice of Jehovah thy God, to observe to do all his commandments which I command thee this day, that Jehovah thy God will set thee on high above all the nations of the earth.

Hebrews 13:17

Obey them that have the rule over you, and submit to them: for they watch in behalf of your souls, as they that shall give account; that they may do this with joy, and not with grief: for this were unprofitable for you.

John 14:23

Jesus answered and said unto him, If a man love me, he will keep my word: and my Father will love him, and we will come unto him, and make our abode with him.

Proverbs 6:20

My son, keep the commandment of thy father, And forsake not the law of thy mother:

Titus 3:1

Put them in mind to be in subjection to rulers, to authorities, to be obedient, to be ready unto every good work,

PATIENCE

James 1:2-4

(2) Count it all joy, my brethren, when ye fall into manifold temptations; (3) knowing that the proving of your faith work patience. (4) And let patience have its perfect work, that ye may be perfect and entire, lacking in nothing.

Psalm 37:7

Rest in Jehovah, and wait patiently for him: Fret not thyself because of him who prosper in his way, Because of the man who bring wicked devices to pass.

Psalm 40:1

I waited patiently for Jehovah; And he inclined unto me, and heard my cry.

PEACE

Colossians 3:15

And let the peace of Christ rule in your hearts, to the which also ye were called in one body; and be ye thankful.

Galatians 5:22

But the fruit of the Spirit is love, joy, peace, long suffering, kindness, goodness, faithfulness

Hebrews 12:14

Follow after peace with all men, and the sanctification without which no man shall see the Lord

James 3:18

And the fruit of righteousness is sown in peace for them that make peace.

John 14:27

Peace I leave with you; my peace I give unto you: not as the world giveth, give I unto you. Let not your heart be troubled, neither let it be fearful.

Romans 5:1

Being therefore justified by faith, we have peace with God through our Lord Jesus Christ;

Psalm 4:8

In peace will I both lay me down and sleep; For thou, Jehovah, alone make me dwell in safety.

Prayer

Colossians 4:2

Continue steadfastly in prayer, watching therein with thanksgiving;

Jeremiah 29:12

And ye shall call upon me, and ye shall go and pray unto me, and I will hearken unto you.

Mark 11:24

Therefore I say unto you, All things whatsoever ye pray and ask for, believe that ye receive them, and ye shall have them.

I John 5:14

And this is the boldness which we have toward him, that, if we ask anything according to his will, he hear us

I Thessalonians 5:17 pray without ceasing;

Reading the Bible

Isaiah 40:8

The grass wither, the flower fade; but the word of our God shall stand forever.

John 5:39

Ye search the scriptures, because ye think that in them ye have eternal life; and these are they which bear witness of me;

Psalm 1:2

But his delight is in the law of Jehovah; And on his law doth he meditate day and night.

Psalm 119:105

Thy word is a lamp unto my feet, And light unto my path.

Romans 15:4

For whatsoever things were written aforetime were written for our learning, that through patience and through comfort of the scriptures we might have hope.

SELF - CONTROL

Galatians 5:22-23

(22) But the fruit of the Spirit is love, joy, peace, long suffering, kindness, goodness, faithfulness, **(23)** meekness, self-control; against such there is no law

Proverbs 25:28

He whose spirit is without restraint Is like a city that is broken down and without walls.

II Peter 1:6

And in your knowledge self-control; and in your self-control patience; and in your patience godliness;

II Timothy 1:7

For God gave us not a spirit of fearfulness; but of power and love and discipline.

I Thessalonians 5:6

So then let us not sleep, as do the rest, but let us watch and be sober.

Serving Others

Acts 26:16

But arise, and stand upon thy feet: for to this end have I appeared unto thee, to appoint thee a minister and a witness both of the things [a]wherein thou hast seen me, and of the things wherein I will appear unto thee

Ephesians 6:7

With good will doing service, as unto the Lord, and not unto men.

Galatians 5:13-14

(13) For ye, brethren, were called for freedom; only use not your freedom for an occasion to the flesh, but through love be servants one to another. **(14)** For the whole law is fulfilled in one word, even in this: Thou shalt love thy neighbor as thyself.

Mark 10:44 - 45

(44) and whosoever would be first among you, shall be servant of all. **(45)** For the Son of man also came not to be ministered unto, but to minister, and to give his life a ransom for many.

Matthew 23:11

But he that is greatest among you shall be your servant.

Sharing Faith

Mark 16:15-16

(15) And he said unto them, Go ye into all the world, and preach the gospel to the whole creation. **(16)** He that believe and is baptized shall be saved; but he that disbelieve shall be condemned.

Matthew 10:19-20

(19) But when they deliver you up, be not anxious how or what ye shall speak: for it shall be given you in that hour what ye shall speak. **(20)** For it is not ye that speak, but the Spirit of your Father that speak in you.

Philemon 6

That the fellowship of thy faith may become effectual, in the knowledge of every good thing which is in you, unto Christ.

Proverbs 11:30

The fruit of the righteous is a tree of life; And he that is wise wins souls.

I Corinthians 9:16

For if I preach the gospel, I have nothing to glory of; for necessity is laid upon me; for woe is unto me, if I preach not the gospel.

SINCERITY

Philemon 10

I beseech thee for my child, whom I have begotten in my bonds, Onesimus,

I Timothy 1:5

But the end of the charge is love out of a pure heart and a good conscience and faith unfeigned

I. Peter 1:22

Seeing ye have purified your souls in your obedience to the truth unto unfeigned love of the brethren, love one another [a]from the heart fervently

II. Corinthians 1:12

For our glorying is this, the testimony of our conscience, that in holiness and sincerity of God, not in fleshly wisdom but in the grace of God, we behaved ourselves in the world, and more abundantly to you-ward

TRUST

Philippians 1:6

I am sure of this, that He who started a good work in you will carry it on to completion until the day of Christ Jesus.

Psalm 27:14

Wait for Jehovah: Be strong, and let thy heart take courage; Yea, wait thou for Jehovah.

Psalm 37:3 - 5

(3) Trust in the Lord and do what is good; dwell in the land and live securely. **(4)** Take delight in the Lord, and He will give you your heart's desires. **(5)** Commit your way to the Lord; trust in Him, and He will act.

Psalm 118:8 8

It is better to take refuge in the Lord than to trust in man.

Proverbs 3:5

Trust in the Lord with all your heart, and do not rely on your own understanding;

Proverbs 28:25

He that is of a greedy spirit stir up strife; But he that put his trust in Jehovah shall be made fat.

TRUTH

John 8:32 and ye shall know the truth, and the truth shall make you free.

John 14:6

Jesus told him, "I am the way, the truth, and the life. No one comes to the Father except through Me.

John 18:37

Pilate therefore said unto him, Art thou a king then? Jesus answered, [a] Thou sayest that I am a king. To this end have I been born, and to this end am I come into the world, that I should bear witness unto the truth. Every one that is of the truth hear my voice.

Psalm 86:15

But You, Lord, are a compassionate and gracious God, slow to anger and rich in faithful love and truth.

Psalm 117:2

For His faithful love to us is great; the Lord's faithfulness endures forever.

Victory

Malachi 4:3

And ye shall tread down the wicked; for they shall be ashes under the soles of your feet in the day that I make, saith Jehovah of hosts.

Psalm 44:5

Through thee will we push down our adversaries: Through thy name will we tread them under that rise up against us.

Revelation 15:2

And I saw as it were a sea of glass mingled with fire; and them that come off victorious from the beast, and from his image, and from the number of his name, standing by the sea of glass, having harps of God.

I John 5:4

For whatsoever is begotten of God overcome the world: and this is the victory that hath overcome the world, even our faith.

Wisdom

Ephesians 1:17

That the God of our Lord Jesus Christ, the Father of glory, may give unto you a spirit of wisdom and revelation in the knowledge of him

James 1:5

But if any of you lack wisdom, let him ask of God, who giveth to all liberally and upbraid not; and it shall be given him

Proverbs 1:5

a wise man will listen and increase his learning, and a discerning man will obtain guidance

Proverbs 2:6

(6) For the Lord gives wisdom; from His mouth come knowledge and understanding.

Psalm 111:10

The fear of the Lord is the beginning of wisdom; all who follow His instructions have good insight. His praise endures forever.

WORSHIP

John 4:23

But an hour is coming, and is now here, when the true worshipers will worship the Father in spirit and truth. Yes, the Father wants such people to worship Him.

Psalm 29:2

Ascribe to Yahweh the glory due His name; worship Yahweh in the splendor of His holiness.

Psalm 95:6

Come, let us worship and bow down; let us kneel before the Lord our Maker.

Psalm 100:2

Serve Jehovah with gladness: Come before his presence with singing.

I Corinthians 14:26

What is it then, brethren? When ye come together, each one hath a psalm, hath a teaching, hath a revelation, hath a tongue, hath an interpretation. Let all things be done unto edifying.

PRAYERS

PRAYER 1

Genesis 37:1 - 11

God we thank you for the love and favor you extend to us who believe in Jesus Christ. We confess that we do not deserve your overwhelming grace towards sinners like us. We praise you though for choosing to make us new creations through our union in Christ's death and resurrection. Please turn us from evil thoughts and worldly distractions diverting our attention from you. Allow the Holy Spirit to open up our eyes to clearly see your revelation in the Bible every day. Help us to learn from the examples of men and women that you have given us in your Word so that we might live more holy lives for your glory. Use your Church here and around the globe to shine brightly for our dark world. We pray all this in the name of Jesus Christ and for his sake, Amen.

PRAYER 2

Genesis 37:12 - 36

God we praise you for your compassionate heart. Give us the relentlessness of the good shepherd who goes after wandering sheep and never gives up. Protect us by your Holy Spirit from being easily discouraged and grant us the spiritual strength to endure the hardships we face. Please deliver us from a sour compulsive nature to envy others and resist your will. Save us from a life of pretense and guard us from using religion as a mask to cover up our resistance to the claims of Jesus Christ on our lives. Father God, please help us during the seasons of grief and loss that we may endure to know that your Son lives, and that in him sorrow can never have the final word. We pray all this in the name of Jesus and for his sake, Amen.

PRAYER 3

Genesis 39:1 - 6

Father God we are grateful for all that you've lavishly blessed us with through our union with Jesus Christ. We praise you for sealing us as your adopted children and making us rich inheritors of your everlasting kingdom. We thank you for comforting us in our moments of weakness and tribulation with the assured knowledge that like Christ you will raise us to life after death. We glorify you for the success that you have given to the Church as the Holy Spirit leads us to proclaim the good news to every tribe, every tongue, and every nation. Lord, we confess that we have often wasted and squandered your blessings. Please forgive us and help us to invest every blessing we have for your kingdom so that you might use us as blessings to others. If it be your will, we ask that you help us to win the favor of our family, friends, and co-workers by unashamedly living out our lives for the gospel and the glory of our Lord Jesus Christ. We pray all this in his name and for his sake, Amen.

PRAYER 4

Genesis 39:6 - 12

Father God we praise you for your absolute goodness, perfection, and holiness. We thank you for your Son, Jesus Christ, who was tempted in every way as we are and yet did not sin. We confess that in our weakness, we have shamefully enjoyed sins of the mind and body that we ought to have resisted. Please forgive us for our unholy failures. Teach us to truly mourn our offenses against you and lead us by the Holy Spirit into faithful repentance. We are grateful for the overwhelming grace that we continue to experience each day because of Jesus' death and resurrection. Thank you for giving us the power of the Holy Spirit to face future temptations. Continue to sanctify us in our frail bodies as we eagerly await the return of your glorified Son. In a world full of darkness, make us your holy lights and gospel witnesses this week. It is the name of Jesus Christ and for his sake that we pray, Amen.

PRAYER 5

Genesis 39:13 - 23

Lord, we praise you for your righteousness and perfect judgments, for you are an incorruptible judge far greater than any corruptible government or sinful man. You are infinitely wise, truly knowing the thoughts, intentions, and hearts of every being that you have ever made. We thank you promising to one day vindicate every lie, every betrayal, and every injustice that your Church endures. Please deliver us from a bitter spirit that so easily becomes resentment and hate when we feel wronged by others. Help us to see your divine purpose and trust in your goodness even in our own suffering and loss. Forgive us for the times when we suppress the truth of your promises and turn to go our own way. By your Holy Spirit, lead us into repentance, guard us from temptation, and sanctify us for your kingdom work among our family, friends, and co-workers this week. Teach us more of the love of Christ that goes on loving even when it is slighted. It is the name of our Lord and Savior Jesus that we pray, Amen.

PRAYER 6

Genesis 41:1 - 43

Father God, we praise you for the Holy Spirit who grants us wisdom, fills us with life, guards our hearts, and illuminates our mind to comprehend the good news of Jesus Christ. Let us settle for nothing less than the pure unadulterated truth that you have revealed to us in your Holy Word. For we confess that apart from you we can do nothing. So please forgive us for the ways in which we have disobeyed your Word to put our own selfish desires before the needs of others. By the Holy Spirit we ask that you lead us into repentance and a life that glorifies you. Help us to resist the allure of this world's deceitful philosophies promising hollow pleasures that ultimately lead to death and destruction. Put a deep desire in our hearts to know the wisdom of the Bible and use it to transform and renew our mind. Use each one of us to exemplify your holiness and love to this world as we aspire to follow Jesus and put his commands into action. Make us your gospel lights this week to those wandering in darkness among our families, friends, neighbors, and co-workers. Embolden us as well as our brothers and sisters across the world to unashamedly proclaim our faith in Jesus Christ. Use our testimonies for your glory to help save souls. All this we pray in the name of Jesus, Amen.

PRAYER 7

Ephesians 3:14-20

A Prayer for the Ephesians

(14) For this reason I kneel before the Father, **(15)** from whom every family in heaven and on earth derives its name. **(16)** I pray that out of his glorious riches he may strengthen you with power through his Spirit in your inner being, **(17)** so that Christ may dwell in your hearts through faith. And I pray that you, being rooted and established in love, **(18)** may have power, together with all the Lord's holy people, to grasp how wide and long and high and deep is the love of Christ, **(19)** and to know this love that surpasses knowledge that you may be filled to the measure of all the fullness of God. **(20)** Now to him who is able to do immeasurably more than all we ask or imagine, according to his power that is at work within us.

PRAYER 8

Isaiah 53:6

God we praise you for your unfathomable grace. Though we deserved punishment for our sins, you were lavishly merciful to the world. In love and justice you gathered our iniquities, and you laid them upon your Son so that we might be forgiven. Enable us now by your Holy Spirit to turn from our own way in order to follow the way of our Savior, Jesus Christ. Guard us from conceited, self-righteous acts and from apathetic obedience to your commands. For those of us struggling with a spirit of rebellion, resistance, resentment, or doubt, we pray that you would grant them a spirit of peace. Thank you God for sharing with us your overwhelming victory over death. In the name of Jesus Christ and for his sake we pray, Amen.

PRAYER 9

John 11:42

And I knew that thou hearest me always: but because of the multitude that stand around I said it, that they may believe that thou didst send me.

PRAYER 10

Jonah 2:2-9

(2) And he said, I called by reason of mine affliction unto Jehovah, And he answered me; Out of the belly of Sheol cried I,And thou heard my voice. **(3)** For thou didst cast me into the depth, in the heart of the seas, And the flood was round about me; All thy waves and thy billows passed over me. **(4)** And I said, I am cast out from before thine eyes; Yet I will look again toward thy holy temple. **(5)** The waters compassed me about, even to the soul; The deep was round about me; The weeds were wrapped about my head. **(6)** I went down to the bottoms of the mountains; The earth with its bars closed upon me for ever: Yet hast thou brought up my life from the pit, O Jehovah my God. **(7)** When my soul fainted within me, I remembered Jehovah; And my prayer came in unto thee, into thy holy temple. **(8)** They that regard lying vanities Forsake their own mercy. **(9)** But I will sacrifice unto thee with the voice of thanksgiving; I will pay that which I have vowed. Salvation is of Jehovah.

PRAYER 11

Judges 16:28

And Samson called unto Jehovah, and said, O Lord Jehovah, remember me, I pray thee, and strengthen me, I pray thee, only this once, O God, that I may be at once avenged of the Philistines for my two eyes.

PRAYER 12

Luke 2:8 - 20

Father God, we bow before you, and recognize our great need of a Savior. Today we want to lift our hearts and give thanks for Your Son, our Lord, Jesus Christ. We lift our hearts in praise to our Savior, and as your loved children and your redeemed servants, we lay our lives before you in worship. Forgive us our sins, guide us by your Spirit into repentance, and make us bold proclaimers of your Word. We pray all this in the name of Jesus Christ our Lord, Amen.

PRAYER 13

Luke 2:22 - 35

Father God we praise you for the ultimate gift of love in your Son. What a marvelous light of hope you have given to our dark world. We thank you for fulfilling your law perfectly in Jesus Christ when not one of us could. We confess that we cannot save ourselves, and we are grateful for the good news of salvation in Christ alone. Please embolden us with the Holy Spirit like Elizabeth, Simeon, and the shepherds to bear witness to Jesus. It is in his name and for his sake that we pray, Amen.

PRAYER 14

Luke 18:13

"God, have mercy on me, a sinner."

PRAYER 15

Luke 1:46 - 49

(46) And Mary said, My soul doth magnify the Lord, **(47)** And my spirit hath rejoiced in God my Savior. **(48)** For he hath looked upon the low estate of his handmaid: For behold, from henceforth all generations shall call me blessed. **(49)** For he that is mighty hath done to me great things; And holy is his name.

PRAYER 16

Matthew 6:9-13 The Lords Prayers

(9) "This, then, is how you should pray: "Our Father in heaven, hallowed be your name, **(10)** your kingdom come, your will be done, on earth as it is in heaven. **(11)** Give us today our daily bread. **(12)** And forgive us our debts, as we also have forgiven our debtors. **(13)** And lead us not into temptation, but deliver us from the evil one."

PRAYER 17

Philippians 1:9 - 11

(9) And this is my prayer: that your love may abound more and more in knowledge and depth of insight, **(10)** so that you may be able to discern what is best and may be pure and blameless for the day of Christ, **(11)** filled with the fruit of righteousness that comes through Jesus Christ to the glory and praise of God.

PRAYER 18

Psalms 23

A psalm of David.

(1) The Lord is my shepherd, I lack nothing. **(2)** He makes me lie down in green pastures, he leads me beside quiet waters **(3)** he refreshes my soul. He guides me along the right paths for his name's sake. **(4)** Even though I walk through the darkest valley, I will fear no evil, for you are with me; your rod and your staff, they comfort me. **(5)** You prepare a table before me in the presence of my enemies. You anoint my head with oil; my cup overflows. **(6)** Surely your goodness and love will follow me all the days of my life, and I will dwell in the house of the Lord forever.

PRAYER 19

Psalm 25:1 - 6

David's Prayer For Guidance

(1) In you, Lord my God I put my trust. **(2)** I trust in you; do not let me be put to shame, nor let my enemies triumph over me. **(3)** No one who hopes in you will ever be put to shame, but shame will come on those who are treacherous without cause. **(4)** Show me your ways, Lord, teach me your paths. **(5)** Guide me in your truth and teach me, for you are God my Savior, and my hope is in you all day long. **(6)** Remember, Lord, your great mercy and love, for they are from of old.Davids Prayer of Repentance

PRAYER 20

Psalm 51:10-12

(10) Create in me a pure heart, O God, and renew a steadfast spirit within me. **(11)** Do not cast me from your presence or take your Holy Spirit from me. **(12)** Restore to me the joy of your salvation and grant me a willing spirit, to sustain me.

PRAYER 21

Psalms 91

(1) Whoever dwells in the shelter of the Most High will rest in the shadow of the Almighty. **(2)** I will say of the Lord, "He is my refuge and my fortress, my God, in whom I trust." **(3)** Surely he will save you from the fowler's snare and from the deadly pestilence. **(4)** He will cover you with his feathers, and under his wings you will find refuge; his faithfulness will be your shield and rampart. **(5)** You will not fear the terror of night, nor the arrow that flies by day, **(6)** nor the pestilence that stalks in the darkness, nor the plague that destroys at midday. **(7)** A thousand may fall at your side, ten thousand at your right hand, but it will not come near you. **(8)** You will only observe with your eyes and see the punishment of the wicked. **(9)** If you say, "The Lord is my refuge,"and you make the Most High your dwelling, **(10)** no harm will overtake you, no disaster will come near your tent. **(11)** For he will command his angels concerning you to guard you in all your ways; **(12)** they will lift you up in their hands, so that you will not strike your foot against a stone. **(13)** You will tread on the lion and the cobra; you will trample the great lion and the serpent. **(14)** "Because he loves me," says the Lord, "I will rescue him; I will protect him, for he acknowledges my name. **(15)** He will call on me, and I will answer him; I will be with him in trouble, I will deliver him and honor him. **(16)**

With long life I will satisfy him and show him my salvation."

PRAYER 22

Psalms 121: 1 - 8

(1) I lift up my eyes to the mountains where does my help come from? **(2)** My help comes from the Lord, the Maker of heaven and earth. **(3)** He will not let your foot slip he who watches over you will not slumber; **(4)** indeed, he who watches over Israel will neither slumber nor sleep. **(5)** The Lord watches over you the Lord is your shade at your right hand; **(6)** the sun will not harm you by day, nor the moon by night. **(7)** The Lord will keep you from all harm he will watch over your life; **(8)** the Lord will watch over your coming and going both now and forevermore.

PRAYER 23

Romans 5:1-11

Father God, we thank you that your amazing unfathomable love has been poured out for us at the cross and poured into us by the Holy Spirit. We want to taste and experience more of the depth and breadth and length and height of your amazing love. Help us to walk by faith. Help us to endure in suffering. Help us to own our need of you. Help us to fully embrace your Son, Jesus Christ, our Redeemer. So, pour out your love into our hearts, in increasing measure by the power of your Holy Spirit, through Jesus Christ our Lord. It is in his name that we pray, Amen.

PRAYER 24

I Chronicles 4:10

And Jabez called on the God of Israel, saying, Oh that thou wouldest bless me indeed, and enlarge my border, and that thy hand might be with me, and that thou wouldest keep me from evil, that it be not to my sorrow! And God granted him that which he requested.

PRAYER 25

II Corinthians 5:1 - 5

Father God, we praise you for the wonderful future that you have prepared for us through the death and resurrection of you Son, Jesus Christ. We eagerly await the day when we will enter into your presence for all eternity with holy bodies untainted by sin. Please help us to not lose heart when we face the many pressures, anxieties, and troubles of life in this fallen world. Let us take great courage in the knowledge that you've given us the Holy Spirit to prepare our souls for our kingdom dwelling with you.

Thank you for letting Jesus live in us. It is in his name that we pray, Amen.

PRAYER 26

II Corinthians 5:6-10

Father God, we praise you for using us to bring joy to your Son, Jesus Christ. In the midst of all the struggles, pressures, and discouragement we face while in our frail, failing bodies, please continue transforming us into servants who are always of good courage. Lead us by your Holy Spirit to find rest in the grand promises that you've revealed to us in your Word. We confess that we are weak and that we need your help. Prepare us for the day when you will judge an account of all our works and offenses. Though we do not deserve your grace, we cannot even begin to express our gratitude for nailing our guilt and shame upon the cross through your crucified Son. Lord, we earnestly long to experience the moment when you will declare to us, "Well done good and faithful servant, enter into the joy of your master." Help us this week as we continue our walk of faith looking forward to the day when our faith will become sight. It is in the name of Jesus that we pray, Amen.

PRAYER 27

II Corinthians 5:11 - 13

We praise you God for your infinite wisdom. We know so little, and yet we are so grateful to serve the one who knows all things. We confess that our hearts have been shattered by our sinful desires, and that we have tried to hide our shame from you. Please forgive us for the ways we've slandered other people in our lives. Our hearts are broken and we cannot save ourselves. We thank you for knowing our own hearts better than we do. We thank you for saving us through your Son, Jesus Christ. We thank you for bringing our dead hearts to life through the power of the Holy Spirit. Please guard our hearts from a critical spirit, and help us to not lose heart when we feel pressures leading us into doubt. Renew our minds and give us confidence with the truth found in the words of the Bible. It is in the name of Jesus Christ that I pray, Amen.

PRAYER 28

II Corinthians 5:14 - 15

Father God, we praise you for the confidence you give our hearts through the love of your Son. We look forward to the day when we will not pass from this world into condemnation, but instead will enter into your presence of everlasting celebration. Father, we confess that we are tired of living for ourselves. We thank you for sending Jesus to die in our place to deliver us from the misery of a self-centered life. No matter what struggles, temptations, or tragedies we face this week, please help us not to lose heart. Through the Holy Spirit, guard us from ever doubting your great love for us. Help us to remember the good news that you have made us your own and that you have forgiven our sins. Lead us to live our lives for Christ's sake at our workplaces, with our friends and families, and wherever else we may go this week. We pray all this in the name of our Lord and Savior, Jesus Christ, Amen.

PRAYER 29

II Corinthians 5:16 - 17

Father God, we praise you for making us new creations in Christ! We are grateful for the good news that you do not regard us by our flesh. We are thankful that unlike us, you know and judge us rightly by our hearts. We are sorry for the ways that we have let our shallow, worldly judgments of others become barriers to our proclamation of your gospel. Thank you for overcoming our weakness and partiality to bring life to our hearts through the Holy Spirit. Please help us to see people more like you do so that we would grow in our boldness to share the gospel with others. We pray all this in Jesus' name, Amen.

PRAYER 30

II Corinthians 5:18 - 20

Father God we thank you for reconciling us through Jesus Christ, and we praise you for choosing to make redeemed sinners like us your gospel ambassadors to this broken world. Please continue to equip us and use us in your redemptive mission as you graciously bring peace to sinners. Sanctify us for your glory as we confess, repent of, and remember the trespasses that we've committed against you. Keep us all humble as we seek reconciliation with other people we've wronged. Protect us with the Holy Spirit from our spirit of pride whenever we serve our families, our church, our coworkers, or strangers in need. Though we don't deserve your forgiveness, we praise you for the unfathomable love and grace that you demonstrate at the cross. Please nourish our hearts daily this week with the words of the Bible and give us courage to proclaim your gospel boldly to all. We pray all this in the name of Jesus and for his sake. Amen.

PRAYER 31

II Corinthians 5:21

Father God we praise you for your perfect righteousness. There is no fairer nor more merciful a judge than you, and we confess that we do not deserve your forgiveness for the sins we've committed. Though we have wronged you, betrayed you, and hated you in so many ways, we thank you for the unbelievable gift of freedom from the power of sin in our lives. Help us to always remember the cost of our freedom and to never forget how Jesus has dealt with our sins at the cross. Help us to also grow in our awareness of the sins that taint our lives so that we would learn to hate our sins like you do. Shine the light of your Holy Spirit into the dark places of our hearts so that we might better know and repent of our sins for your glory. Thank you so much for reconciling us through the gospel to make us your righteous servants. Use us to proclaim your good news boldly to others this week. We pray all this in the name of Jesus and for his sake,

Amen.

PRAYER 32

I Chronicles 4:10

Jabez cried out to the God of Israel, "Oh, that you would bless me and enlarge my territory! Let your hand be with me, and keep me from harm so that I will be free from pain." And God granted his request.